My Spectacular Self

Out-of-Control Rhino

An Impulse Control Story

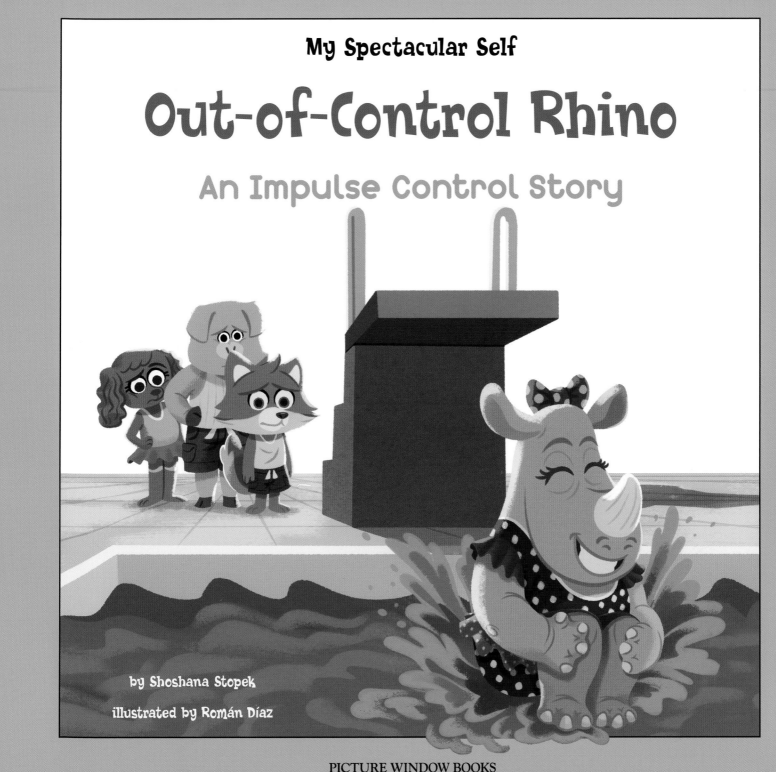

by Shoshana Stopek

illustrated by Román Díaz

PICTURE WINDOW BOOKS

a capstone imprint

For anyone who's ever felt a little
out of control, you got this. —S.S.

Published by Picture Window Books, an imprint of Capstone
1710 Roe Crest Drive, North Mankato, Minnesota 56003
capstonepub.com

Library of Congress Cataloging-in-Publication Data
Names: Stopek, Shoshana, author. | Díaz, Román (Illustrator), illustrator.
Title: Out-of-control rhino : an impulse control story / by Shoshana Stopek ;
illustrated by Román Díaz.
Description: North Mankato, Minnesota : Picture Window Books, [2022] |
Series: My spectacular self | Audience: Ages 5-7 | Audience: Grades K-1 |
Summary: Roxy the Rhino does not mean to interrupt or cut in line but after meeting
a new friend she learns to control her impulses and stop and think before acting.
Identifiers: LCCN 2021028468 | ISBN 9781663984883 (hardcover) | ISBN 9781666332483
(paperback) | ISBN 9781666332490 (pdf) | ISBN 9781666332513 (kindle edition)
Subjects: CYAC: Rhinoceroses—Fiction. | Self-control—Fiction. | Friendship—Fiction.
Classification: LCC PZ7.1.S7557 Ou 2022 | DDC [E]—dc23
LC record available at https://lccn.loc.gov/2021028468

Special thanks to Amber Chandler for her consulting work.

Designed by Nathan Gassman

Printed and bound in the United States of America. PO4608

Meet Roxy

HOBBIES: swimming, bike riding, ballet, hanging out with friends

FAVORITE BOOKS: Rhino Dance Party and Waiting is Tough Stuff

FAVORITE FOOD: chocolate fudge brownie ice cream sundae with whipped cream and cherries

FUTURE GOALS: become a famous dancer or a rock star

GOALS FOR THIS YEAR:
* BE MORE PATIENT
* LISTEN MORE
* USE MY LIBRARY VOICE
* PERFECT MY PLIÉ

Summer vacation was in full swing, and Roxy was excited to show off her new bathing suit. She strutted to the front of the line and did her best cannonball.

When she got out of the pool, she ran into another rhino.

"Epic cannonball," he said.

"Thanks," said Roxy. "I like to make a BIG splash whenever I can."

"I'm Randy. I'm new in town."

"I'm Roxy. Let's go on the high dive!"

"There's a long line," Randy pointed out.

"Who has time for lines?" asked Roxy, making a beeline for the front.

After swimming, Roxy took her new friend around town.

"That's where I go to school . . .

That's where I learned how to swim . . .

Oh! That's where I take ballet.
I totally ROCK a tutu."

Roxy had so much to say that Randy couldn't get a word in.

Then they went to Roxy's favorite ice cream shop.
Roxy ordered a cone with chocolate fudge brownie
and caramel swirl ice cream topped with sprinkles,
whipped cream, a twizzle stick, and a cherry.

Randy ordered plain vanilla.

"Mmm, this is delicious!" declared Roxy. "But it still needs a little something." She grabbed a spoonful of Randy's ice cream.

Roxy had a feeling she should have asked, but it just looked so tempting that it was hard to hold back.

The next day, Roxy was invited to Randy's house.
His room was nice and clean and filled with games.
Roxy grabbed one and dumped it out, but Randy
wanted to show her something else.

"I used to have a hard time being patient," he said. "At my old school, I learned a rhyme called the Stop, Think, and Wink. It helps me to remember to stop and think before I act."

"But I don't like to miss out on the fun.
There isn't enough time to stop and wait
around. And I'm already amazing at winking,"
Roxy replied.

BEFORE YOU ACT,
STOP AND THINK.
TAKE A DEEP BREATH,
AND FINISH
WITH A WINK.

Randy seemed a little hurt. "You ARE great at winking.
I just thought you might want to learn the rhyme too."

"Well, I don't know when I'd use it," Roxy said.
"See ya later!"

BEFORE YOU ACT,
STOP AND THINK.
TAKE A DEEP BREATH,
AND FINISH
WITH A WINK.

On her way home, Roxy stopped at the library.
There was a super long line at the checkout.

Roxy was about to cut when she thought about the
Stop, Think, and Wink. She STOPPED, took a deep
BREATH, and WAITED. It wasn't easy, but she did it!

After that, Roxy used the Stop, Think, and Wink
as much as she could.

At the pool, the park, the library, and at a birthday party, Roxy used the helpful rhyme.

By the time she saw Randy again, Roxy had so much to tell him she thought she might BURST! They both started talking at the EXACT same time.

Then Roxy remembered the Stop, Think, and Wink.

"I have an idea," said Roxy. "Let's take turns."

They both got their moment to talk AND to listen.

They both got a chance to go first AND were patient when it wasn't their turn.

And, best of all, they SHARED.

And whenever Roxy used her new trick, it was ALWAYS worth the wait.

Stop, Think, and Wink

Impulse control is the ability to control yourself, especially your emotions and actions. New situations or when you have to wait a long time or sit still can make it really tough to control yourself.

When you feel out of control, recite Roxy and Randy's rhyme about impulse control. Think about what you will say or do, then go with the best choice and be the best you!

Before you act,
stop and think.
Take a deep breath,
and finish with a wink.

Impulse Control Matters

1. When is a time when you just couldn't be quiet, even if you were supposed to?

2. Can you pretend to "zip your lips" or "lock your mouth and throw away the key?" When are times that you need to practice being quiet, even if you don't want to?

3. Here is a trick to calm your insides down. It is called 4-7-8 breathing. Breathe in through your nose while you count to four in your head. Then, hold it for seven seconds. Finally, blow out for eight seconds, making a whooshing sound. How does this make you feel?

4. How do you feel when someone is very excitable near you? Sometimes it can be fun to get excited. Sometimes it can make you feel nervous or anxious. What is a nice way to tell someone to calm down?

5. It is helpful to think of a very slow-moving animal when you have the wiggles. What are some slow animals? Can you act like one? Try being a sloth!

About the Author

Shoshana Stopek is the author of numerous books for kids and grown-ups. Her picture book series My Spectacular Self includes *Hammock for Two, Out-of-Control Rhino, Heads Up!*, and *Sometimes Cows Wear Polka Dots*. Shoshana grew up in New Jersey, where she learned how to make new friends, fly a kite, and bedazzle a wardrobe. Now she lives in Los Angeles with her husband and daughter where she writes and occasionally still bedazzles. Visit her at shoshanastopek.com.

About the Illustrator

Román Díaz was born in Mexico. Since he was a child, he always wanted to draw like adults. Now that he is an adult he likes to draw like children. He's created illustrations for books, video games, and many other projects. He likes to eat colorful fruits and vegetables and admires animals in documentaries because it seems they have superpowers.